Ali Baba and the Forty Thieves

Retold by Katie Daynes

Illustrated by
Paddy Mounter

Reading Consultant: Alison Kelly
Roehampton University

Contents

Chapter 1

A secret cave

Long ago in Persia, there lived
two brothers. Kasim was a
rich merchant, but Ali Baba
was only a poor woodcutter.

While Kasim ran a large store in town, Ali Baba spent his time collecting firewood. He would gather twigs and branches to sell at the market.

It's a hard life.

One day, Ali Baba spotted a band of horsemen galloping into the woods. They had daggers and looked dangerous. Quickly, he hid in a tree.

The men stopped at a cliff near Ali Baba's tree.

"Open, Sesame!" cried their leader and a hole appeared in the rock. Silently, they went in.

"That's amazing!" thought Ali Baba. He wanted to explore but he was scared of the men.

After a long wait, he saw the rock open again. He counted the men as they hurried out. There were 40 of them!

"Shut, Sesame," said their leader. The rock closed and the men rode away.

Follow me, men.

Ali Baba slid down from his tree. He tried the magic words. "Open, Sesame?" Instantly, the rock opened. Ali Baba crept inside and gasped. The cave was crammed with treasure.

7

"Those men must be thieves!" he thought. "They won't miss a few coins..." And he filled four bags with gold.

He turned to go, but the rock had closed behind him.

"Open, Sesame!" he cried. The rock slid open and he darted out. "Shut, Sesame," he added, before racing home.

Ali Baba's wife was stunned to see his bags full of gold instead of wood.

"I must be dreaming," she sighed. Then Ali Baba told her the whole story.

"We should hide the gold," she said. "But first let's find out how rich we are!"

She ran to Kasim's house and asked to borrow his wife's scales. Kasim's wife wondered why. Secretly, she smeared some wax on the scales before handing them over.

Thank you.

When the scales came back, Kasim's wife found a gold coin stuck to the wax. She showed it to Kasim.

"Your brother isn't a poor man after all!" she cried.

He weighs his gold!

The next day, Kasim took the coin to Ali Baba.

"Tell me where this came from!" he ordered.

Ali Baba couldn't lie to his brother. So he told him about the cave.

Chapter 2

The thieves return

"Gold, eh?" thought Kasim.
He hired ten donkeys and took
them to the place Ali Baba
had described.

12

"Open, Sesame!" he cried. The rock opened and Kasim stepped into the cave. He was dazzled by all the treasure.

I want... everything!

He stuffed his bags full, then turned to leave. But he'd forgotten the magic words.

"Open, ss... ss... Strawberry!" he cried. Nothing happened.

Kasim was trapped. Worse still, he could hear voices outside. He wanted to hide, but he was frozen with fear. Suddenly the rock opened.

"Get him, men!" shouted the leader of the thieves. "He knows our secret. Chop him up and leave his body to scare other people away."

14

That night, Kasim didn't come home for supper. His wife was worried. She went to Ali Baba's house in tears.

"I think Kasim's in trouble," she wailed. "Please find him."

Morning came and there
was still no sign of Kasim. Ali
Baba went to look in the cave.

"Open, Sesame!" he called.
The rock slid back to reveal a
horrible sight. Kasim's body
lay in four pieces.

Ali Baba quickly put them
in a bag and hurried home.

"I can't bury my brother in pieces!" he thought. He went to ask Kasim's loyal servant, Morgiana, for help.

I know just the man for the job.

Morgiana went straight to Mustafa the tailor.

"I need you to sew up something in secret," she said. "I'll pay you well, but you must let me blindfold you."

17

Mustafa agreed – he needed the money. Morgiana led him to Ali Baba's house and made him sew up Kasim's body.

Soon Ali Baba was able to bury his brother in one piece. He pretended that Kasim had died of an illness.

Chapter 3

"X" marks the spot

Meanwhile, the thieves had more stolen goods to hide.

"Gamal, the body's gone!" cried a thief to their leader.

19

"Someone else must know about our cave!" Gamal replied. "We must kill him too."

"Let me go to town and track down our enemy," suggested one of the thieves.

OK. But be careful.

The thief was in town before sunrise. Only Mustafa the tailor was already at work.

20

"How can you sew in the dark?" asked the thief.

"It's easy," replied the tailor. "The other day I even sewed up a body while blindfolded!"

"A body!" said the thief. "I'll give you a gold coin if you show me where you did that."

But Mustafa couldn't remember the way. So the thief put a blindfold on him. "Now can you find the house?" he asked.

An hour later, Morgiana arrived at Ali Baba's house from the market.

"What's this cross for?" she wondered. "I think something fishy is going on..."

She drew crosses on the doors of nine other houses, so Ali Baba's didn't stand out.

Back at the cave, the thief was telling his friends about Mustafa and the house.

"I can show you where our enemy lives," he said.

He took Gamal to Ali Baba's street... only to find ten doors marked instead of one.

Gamal returned to the cave, very annoyed.

"Right," he said. "I'll give a sack of jewels to the man who can find our enemy."

I'll do it!

And so a different thief set off to ask for Mustafa's help.

When they reached the door, the thief had an idea.

"I'll mark it in *red* chalk!" he thought.

After he'd left, Morgiana noticed the new cross. She quickly drew nine more – in red this time.

The second thief led Gamal to Ali Baba's street. There were so many crosses, he didn't know where to start.

"Must I do everything myself?" cried Gamal.

Chapter 4

The oil seller

Before long, Gamal had
hatched a plan. First, he
ordered his men to buy 38
big oil jars and 19 donkeys.

He filled one jar with oil and left the rest empty.

"I want 37 of you to hide in the jars," he told his men.

Then he disguised himself as an oil seller and led the donkeys into town. Each donkey carried two jars.

Gamal went to see Mustafa. "Show me where you sewed up that body," he said, giving Mustafa three gold coins.

Here we are.

Thanks. You can go now.

At Ali Baba's door, Gamal knocked loudly.

"Can I help?" said Ali Baba.

"I hope so," replied Gamal. "I'm an honest oil seller, with nowhere to stay..."

"Well, come in and make yourself at home," said Ali Baba. "You can leave your donkeys in the yard."

While Gamal unloaded his jars, he spoke to the thieves.

"Keep hidden until I throw a pebble from my window," he whispered. "Then you know it's time to attack."

Morgiana was preparing supper for Ali Baba and his guest when her lamp ran out of oil.

"I'm sure the oil seller won't mind if I take some of his," she thought.

She reached the first jar, and was shocked to hear a voice.

"Is it time, Gamal?" it asked.

Thinking quickly, she replied in a deep voice, "No, not yet." Then she went from jar to jar, listening for voices.

Only one jar contained oil. Men were hiding in the others.

33

Morgiana guessed Ali Baba was in big trouble. She took the oil to the kitchen, heated it in a huge pot, then carried it out to the yard. Carefully, she tipped sizzling oil into all 37 jars. One by one, the thieves spluttered and died.

That night, Gamal looked out of his window.
"All clear," he thought and threw a pebble at one of the jars.

Twenty pebbles later, there was still no sign of his men.
"They must be asleep," he thought and crept outside to wake them.

To his horror,
he found all
his men dead!
He panicked
and fled.

In the morning, Morgiana
showed Ali Baba the dead
men and told him about the
oil seller's escape.

"They're the thieves I saw
at the cave!" he cried. "We'd
better bury them here."

Chapter 5

Revenge

By now, Gamal was very
angry. He thought of nothing
but killing Ali Baba.

37

While he was plotting, he decided to sell some of the treasure. He dressed up as a businessman and set up a market stall.

By chance, Ali Baba's nephew ran a stall nearby.

The two men got along well. "I've made a new friend," the nephew told Ali Baba.

A week later, Ali Baba's wife held a dinner party for their nephew and his friend. Gamal found himself face to face with his enemy. All went well... until Ali Baba offered him salt.

In Persia it was very unlucky to harm someone if you'd eaten their salt.

Morgiana heard their guest refuse the salt.

"Strange," she thought, and studied him more closely.

"It's the man who pretended to be an oil seller!" she gasped. "I must protect Ali Baba."

Quickly, she changed into dancing clothes. With a tambourine in her hand and a dagger at her side, she swayed and twirled in front of the party.

Her dance was greeted with claps and cheers.

Again!

Bravo!

Then Morgiana went from one person to the next, holding out her tambourine for money. Ali Baba gave her a coin and so did his nephew.

Gamal fumbled for his purse. "This is my chance," thought Morgiana. As Gamal looked down, she took her dagger and stabbed him.

The others jumped up.
"What have you done?"
cried Ali Baba.
"I've saved your life,"
Morgiana replied.

"Look carefully at your guest," she went on. "He's really the fake oil seller."

"He's also the leader of the thieves!" cried Ali Baba.

He must have been after me ever since I found his cave...

Quickly, they buried Gamal's body with the other thieves.

"Morgiana, how can I ever repay you?" Ali Baba asked.

"Maybe she could marry me..." suggested his nephew.

"Great idea," said Ali Baba. "We'll have the wedding of the year. And there's a cave full of treasure to pay for it."

Who first told this story?

Ali Baba and the Forty Thieves comes from a collection of Arabian stories known as *The Thousand and One Nights*.

According to legend, a Sultan wanted to kill his wife. To save herself, the wife started telling him a wonderful story.

The Sultan found the story so good, he let her live to finish it. Then she started another one. Hundreds of stories and 1001 nights later, the Sultan let his wife go.

Series editor: Lesley Sims

Designed by
Russell Punter

This edition first published in 2007 by Usborne Publishing Ltd.,
Usborne House, 83-85 Saffron Hill, London EC1N 8RT, England.
www.usborne.com
Copyright © 2007, 2003 Usborne Publishing Ltd.

48